RUTH

A MODERN TALE OF LOVE AND LOYALTY

WOMEN OF THE BIBLE FICTION
BOOK 1

KAYLA LOWE

Want a free book? Sign up to my newsletter to get my award-winning book for free! www.authorkaylalowe.com

MORE OF MY BOOKS

<u>Series</u>

<u>Charms of the Chaste Court</u>

A Courtship in Covent Garden
Whispers in Westminster
Romance in Regent's Park
Serenade on Strand Street
Treasure in Tower Bridge

<u>Sweet Honey by the Sea</u>

<u>The Beekeeper's Secret (Book 1)</u>
<u>A Royal Honeycomb (Book 2)</u>
<u>Bees in Blossom (Book 3)</u>
<u>Honeyed Kisses (Book 4)</u>
<u>Blooming Forever (Book 5)</u>

<u>Strawberry Beach Series</u>

<u>Beachside Lessons (Book 1)</u>
<u>Beachside Lessons (Book 2)</u>
<u>Beachside Lessons (Book 3)</u>

Panama City Beach Series

Sun-Kissed Secrets (Book 1)
Sun-Kissed Secrets (Book 2)
Sun-Kissed Secrets (Book 3)

The Tainted Love Saga

Of Love and Deception (Book 1)
Of Love and Family (Book 2)
Of Love and Violence (Book 3)
Of Love and Abuse(Book 4)
Of Love and Crime (Book 5)
Of Love and Addiction (Book 6)
Of Love and Redemption (Book 7)

Standalones

Maiden's Blush

Poetry

Phantom Poetry
Lost and Found

CHAPTER 1

Light filtered through the lace curtains, casting intricate shadows across the faded wallpaper. Ruth sat in the old wooden chair by the window, her hands folded in her lap. She gazed out at the quiet street, the stillness broken only by the occasional rustling of leaves in the gentle breeze. In the silence, memories flooded her mind, carrying her back to the life she had shared with her beloved husband.

She recalled their first meeting, a chance encounter at a bustling coffee shop. His warm smile and kind eyes had drawn her in, sparking a connection that would grow into something beautiful and profound. They had built a life together, navigating the joys and challenges that came their way. Through laughter and tears, triumphs and setbacks, their love had been the constant that anchored them.

But now, in the aftermath of his passing, Ruth found herself adrift, struggling to find her footing in this new reality. The weight of grief pressed heavily upon her heart, a constant companion that shadowed her every step. She yearned for his comforting presence, his gentle touch, and the sound of his voice that had always soothed her troubled soul.

With a sigh, Ruth stood and made her way to the kitchen, her footsteps echoing in the empty house. She opened the cabinet, reaching for a mug, but paused as her fingers brushed against the chipped one he had always favored. A bittersweet smile tugged at her lips as she remembered the countless mornings they had shared, sipping coffee and planning their day.

As she prepared her tea, Ruth's thoughts turned to the pressing matters at hand. The move to this small town had been a necessary step, a chance for her and Naomi to find solace and support in the close-knit community. Yet, the financial challenges loomed large, casting a shadow over their already fragile existence.

Ruth had spent countless hours scouring job

listings, her hope dwindling with each rejection. The skills she had honed in the city seemed of little use here, where opportunities were scarce and competition fierce. She worried for Naomi, who had already endured so much loss, and the burden of providing for them both weighed heavily on her shoulders.

"Lord, please guide me," she whispered, her eyes closing as she leaned against the counter. "Show me the way forward, and grant me the strength to face whatever lies ahead."

As the steam from her tea curled upward, Ruth felt a flicker of determination ignite within her. She had weathered storms before, and with faith and perseverance, she would find a way through this one as well. For Naomi's sake, and for the memory of the love she had shared with her husband, Ruth would not give up.

With renewed resolve, she returned to the window, her gaze fixed on the horizon. The path ahead was uncertain, but Ruth knew that she would face it with the same quiet strength and resilience that had carried her this far. In this new chapter of her life, she would find purpose and hope, guided by the unwavering love that still lived within her heart.

The gentle creak of the floorboards announced Naomi's presence, and Ruth turned to see her mother-in-law's weathered face etched with concern. Naomi's eyes, once bright with joy, now held a shadow of the grief that had become their constant companion. She approached Ruth slowly, her steps measured and heavy, as if the weight of their shared sorrow had settled into her very bones.

"Oh, my dear girl," Naomi murmured, her voice a soothing balm against the silence. She reached out, her work-worn hands clasping Ruth's own, and in that simple gesture, a flicker of warmth passed between them. "I know the road ahead seems daunting, but you mustn't lose heart."

Ruth's throat tightened, emotion threatening to overtake her. She looked down at their intertwined fingers, drawing strength from the connection. "I just...I don't know how to make it right, Naomi. I've tried so hard to find work, to provide for us, but it feels like every door is closed."

Naomi's gaze softened, a sad smile tugging at the corners of her mouth. "You've already done so much, Ruth. More than I could ever have asked." She gently cupped Ruth's cheek, tilting her face upward until their eyes met. "Your love, your loyalty...it's a balm to my weary soul. You are a blessing, and together, we will find our way."

Tears spilled down Ruth's cheeks, and she leaned into Naomi's touch, allowing herself a moment of vulnerability. The weight of their shared grief hung heavy in the air, a palpable presence that seemed to seep into the very walls of their modest home.

"I miss him," Ruth whispered, her voice barely audible. "I miss the life we had, the dreams we shared. And sometimes...sometimes I fear I'll never find that kind of love again."

Naomi drew Ruth into a tight embrace, her own tears mingling with her daughter-in-law's. "Oh, my sweet girl," she murmured, her words muffled against Ruth's hair. "The love you and my son shared...it was a rare and beautiful thing. But I know, with all my heart, that you will find happiness again. You have so much light within you, so much to give."

As they clung to each other, the warmth of Naomi's love enveloped Ruth, a soothing balm against the ache of loss. In that moment, Ruth knew that though their path was marked by sorrow, they would face it together, drawing strength from the unbreakable bond they shared.

And somewhere, deep within her heart, a flicker of hope began to grow, a tiny spark amidst the darkness. For even in the midst of their grief, Ruth knew that the love they had lost would forever be a part of them, guiding them forward into a future where healing and new beginnings awaited.

CHAPTER 2

Naomi's gaze lingered on the faded family photograph, her weathered hands tracing the faces of loved ones now gone. The weight of memories hung heavy in the air, mingling with the scent of lavender from the modest kitchen window. She sighed, a sound that carried the weariness of countless sleepless nights.

"I don't know, Ruth," Naomi began, her voice barely above a whisper. "Starting over at my age...it seems an impossible task." She turned to face her daughter-in-law, searching those gentle green eyes for a glimmer of understanding. "But what choice do we have? The city holds nothing for us now."

Ruth reached out, her warm hand encircling Naomi's. A silent gesture of support, of shared grief and resilience. They had weathered storms together, two women bound by love and loss. In this moment, Ruth felt the depth of their connection, a bond forged in the crucible of adversity.

"We'll make it work, Naomi," Ruth assured her, a quiet determination in her voice. "This community, it's a chance for us to heal, to build something new." She glanced around the humble room, already envisioning the possibilities. A fresh coat of paint, perhaps some potted herbs on the sill. Small touches to make this house a home.

Naomi nodded, drawing strength from Ruth's unwavering optimism. She knew the road ahead would be fraught with challenges, but with Ruth by her side, she dared to hope. To believe that even in the autumn of her life, new beginnings were possible.

As Naomi busied herself in the kitchen, preparing a simple meal, Ruth's ears caught the murmur of conversation drifting through the open window. Naomi's old friends, their voices tinged with excitement, spoke of a man named Boaz. A successful businessman, they said, with a heart of gold. A pillar of the community who went out of his way to help others.

Ruth found herself intrigued, drawn to the idea of a man who embodied such kindness and integrity. In a world that had dealt her more than its fair share of hardships, the notion of goodness felt like a balm to her weary soul. She wondered, fleetingly, if their paths might cross someday.

But for now, her focus remained on Naomi, on building a life in this close-knit community that had welcomed them with open arms. Together, they would navigate the uncertainties of the future, finding solace in each other's presence and the promise of new beginnings.

Ruth entered the kitchen, the aroma of Naomi's cooking enveloping her like a comforting embrace. She watched as her mother-in-law stirred a pot of fragrant stew, her movements measured and precise, yet tinged with an underlying weariness.

"Naomi," Ruth began softly, her voice a gentle invitation to share the burdens weighing on her heart. "I can see the worry in your eyes. Talk to me."

Naomi paused, her gaze fixed on the simmering pot before her. "I just...I wonder if we've made the right decision, staying here." Her words hung heavy in the air, a confession of the doubts that plagued her. "Starting over at my age, with no guarantees...It's daunting."

Ruth stepped closer, placing a reassuring hand

on Naomi's shoulder. "I know it's not easy," she acknowledged, her voice a soothing balm. "But we're in this together, Naomi. Every step of the way."

Naomi turned to face her, eyes glistening with unshed tears. "What if I can't provide for us? What if I'm not strong enough?"

Ruth's heart ached at the vulnerability in Naomi's voice. She knew all too well the weight of uncertainty, the fear of an unknown future. Yet, in that moment, she found within herself a well of strength, a resilience forged in the crucible of her own struggles.

"You are stronger than you know," Ruth assured her, conviction ringing in every word. "And you're not alone. We have each other, and we have faith. God will guide us through this, just as He has guided us here."

Naomi's lips curved into a tremulous smile, a flicker of hope illuminating her careworn features. "You always know just what to say," she murmured, gratitude evident in her tone.

Ruth returned her smile, a silent promise passing between them. Together, they would weather whatever storms lay ahead, finding solace in their shared faith and the unbreakable bond of family.

As they sat down to their modest meal, hearts full of newfound resolve, Ruth couldn't help but let her thoughts drift to the enigmatic Boaz. A man of integrity, respected by all. She wondered what role, if any, he might play in their lives. But for now, she pushed those musings aside, content in the knowledge that, come what may, she and Naomi would face it hand in hand, their love a beacon of light in an uncertain world.

CHAPTER 3

The community center buzzed with chatter as Ruth stepped through the doors, her hand clasped tightly in Naomi's. A sea of unfamiliar faces filled the room, and for a fleeting moment, Ruth felt adrift, a foreigner in this new land she now called home. Warm smiles greeted them, yet behind each friendly expression, Ruth sensed a hint of uncertainty, a subtle distance that underscored her status as an outsider.

Naomi squeezed her hand reassuringly, a gesture that spoke volumes without uttering a word. They navigated the crowded space, exchanging polite greetings and introductions. Ruth's gaze drifted to the colorful posters adorning the walls, each one highlighting various volunteer opportunities and community projects.

"Ruth, this is Pastor David and his wife, Sarah," Naomi said, guiding her towards a middle-aged couple. "Pastor David, Sarah, I'd like you to meet my daughter-in-law, Ruth."

"Welcome, Ruth," Pastor David extended a warm hand, his eyes crinkling at the corners as he smiled. "We're so glad you and Naomi have joined our little community. How are you settling in?"

Ruth returned the handshake, her lips curving into a gentle smile. "Thank you, Pastor. It's been an adjustment, but everyone has been very kind. I'm grateful for the welcome we've received."

As the conversation flowed, Ruth found herself drawn to a flyer pinned to the notice board, its bold letters proclaiming 'Volunteers Needed'. The image of helping hands reaching out to one another stirred something deep within her, a longing to contribute, to find purpose amidst the whirlwind of change.

Excusing herself politely, Ruth approached the notice board, her fingers tracing the words on the flyer. The community center was seeking volunteers for various programs - from tutoring underprivileged children to assisting the elderly. Each opportunity felt like a small beacon of light, a chance to make a difference in the lives of others.

In that moment, Ruth made a decision. She reached for the sign-up sheet, her hand steady as she penned her name under the 'Volunteer' column. It was a small act, a seemingly insignificant choice in the grand scheme of things, yet for Ruth, it held the promise of something more.

As she rejoined Naomi and the others, Ruth felt a flicker of hope ignite within her. Perhaps this was the first step in finding her place, in weaving herself into the tapestry of this close-knit community. She may have been an outsider, but with each passing moment, with each connection forged, Ruth knew she was one step closer to belonging.

Ruth walked into the community center, her heart fluttering with anticipation and nervousness. The warm, inviting atmosphere embraced her as she made her way to the reception desk, where a friendly face greeted her with a smile.

"Hello, I'm Ruth Anderson. I signed up to volunteer," she said, her voice soft but clear.

The receptionist, a middle-aged woman with kind eyes, glanced at the volunteer list and nodded. "Ah, yes, Ruth! We're so glad to have you here. Let me introduce you to Marcus, one of our coordinators. He'll be able to guide you through the different projects we have going on."

As if on cue, a tall, lanky man emerged from a nearby office. His relaxed demeanor and easy grin instantly put Ruth at ease. "Marcus, this is Ruth, our new volunteer," the receptionist introduced.

"Pleasure to meet you, Ruth," Marcus said, extending his hand. "I'm thrilled you've decided to join our little family here."

Ruth shook his hand, feeling the warmth of his welcome. "Thank you. I'm excited to be here and contribute in any way I can."

As they walked through the bustling halls of the community center, Marcus began to share stories about the various programs and initiatives they had underway. Ruth listened intently, her mind already spinning with ideas and possibilities.

"You know," Marcus said, turning to Ruth with a thoughtful expression, "I heard that Boaz Mitchell, the owner of Mitchell's Organic Grocery, is looking for someone to help with a local project he's spearheading. It's all about promoting sustainable living and community engagement."

Ruth's interest piqued at the mention of Boaz's name. She had heard whispers about him, about his dedication to the community and his innovative approach to business. "Really? That sounds fascinating. What kind of project is it?"

Marcus smiled, seeing the spark of enthusiasm in Ruth's eyes. "From what I've heard, he's planning a series of workshops and events to educate people about organic farming, composting, and other eco-friendly practices. He's looking for someone with a background in marketing or communications to help spread the word and get the community involved."

Ruth's heart skipped a beat. Her mind raced with the potential of being a part of something so meaningful, so aligned with her own values. Could this be the opportunity she had been seeking? A chance to use her skills and experience to make a difference?

As they continued their tour of the community center, Ruth's thoughts kept drifting back to Boaz and his project. She couldn't help but feel a sense of excitement, a whisper of possibility that perhaps, just perhaps, this could be the beginning of something extraordinary.

CHAPTER 4

Ruth took a deep breath as she stepped through the doors of Boaz's company, the scent of fresh produce and freshly baked bread enveloping her. The hustle and bustle of the store felt invigorating, a welcome change from the quiet solitude of her new home. As she made her way to the employee break room, Ruth caught sight of Boaz, his presence commanding yet comforting. He greeted her with a warm smile, his eyes crinkling at the corners.

"Ruth, it's wonderful to have you here," Boaz said, his voice rich and sincere. "I know you'll be a valuable addition to our team."

She returned his smile, feeling a flutter of nerves and excitement. "Thank you for the opportunity, Boaz. I'm eager to learn and contribute however I can."

As the day unfolded, Ruth immersed herself in the intricacies of the business, absorbing every detail like a sponge. She marveled at the care and attention given to each product, the way Boaz and his employees treated every customer with kindness and respect. In the midst of the organized chaos, Ruth found a sense of purpose, a glimmer of hope that perhaps this was where she was meant to be.

The days turned into weeks, and Ruth's dedication did not go unnoticed. Boaz often found himself observing her from afar, admiring the way she tackled each task with quiet determination. There was a strength in her gentleness, a resilience that shone through even in the most mundane moments.

In her free time, Ruth found solace in volunteering at the community center, the act of giving back to others a balm for her own healing heart. She poured herself into organizing food drives and reading to children, the smiles on their faces a reminder of the good that still existed in the world.

As she worked side by side with other volunteers, Ruth's kind nature and tireless work ethic earned her the respect and admiration of those around her. They saw in her a woman of substance, someone whose presence brought light to even the darkest of days.

And though the memories of her past still lingered, Ruth began to feel the stirrings of something new, a tentative hope that life could be beautiful again. With each passing day, she grew more certain that this small community, with its big-hearted people, was exactly where she needed to be.

Naomi stood by the window, her gaze wandering over the quaint garden that stretched before their new home. The sun's gentle rays caressed her face, and for the first time in what felt like an eternity, she allowed herself to breathe deeply, savoring the sweet scent of blooming roses and freshly cut grass.

In the quiet moments of the morning, Naomi found herself reflecting on the journey that had brought her here. The loss of her husband and sons had left an indelible mark on her soul, a pain that she once believed would never subside. Yet, as she watched Ruth bustle about the kitchen, humming a soft melody as she prepared breakfast, Naomi felt a flicker of hope reignite within her.

"You know, Ruth," Naomi said, her voice barely above a whisper, "I never thought I'd find peace again. But being here, with you, in this place... it's starting to feel like home."

Ruth turned from the stove, her green eyes shimmering with understanding. She crossed the room, enveloping Naomi in a warm embrace. "I feel it too," she murmured, "It's like we were meant to be here, to start anew."

As they sat down to eat, the conversation flowed easily, punctuated by gentle laughter and shared memories. Naomi found herself speaking of her husband and sons, the love and joy they had brought to her life. The pain of their absence remained, but it was tempered now by the realization that their love lived on within her.

In the days that followed, Naomi began to venture out more, exploring the town and meeting the locals. She discovered a knitting group at the community center, where she could share her skills and connect with others who understood the healing power of crafting. Slowly but surely, she felt the weight of her grief beginning to lift, replaced by a growing sense of belonging.

And as she watched Ruth flourish in her new job and volunteer work, Naomi knew that their decision to start over had been the right one. Together, they were building a life filled with purpose and love, a testament to the resilience of the human spirit.

In the quiet of the evening, as the sun dipped below the horizon, Naomi would often sit on the porch swing, a cup of tea in hand. She'd close her eyes, letting the gentle breeze caress her face, and whisper a prayer of gratitude for the second chance she'd been given. In this small corner of the world, she had found a place to call home, and a love that would guide her through whatever lay ahead.

CHAPTER 5

Ruth stood at the edge of the bustling community event, her eyes scanning the crowd as she adjusted the modest blue dress she wore. The chatter of voices and laughter filled the warm evening air, mingling with the aroma of freshly baked bread from a nearby stall. She took a deep breath, summoning the courage to step into the throng of neighbors and new faces.

As she made her way through the crowd, Ruth's attention was drawn to a booth showcasing handcrafted goods from local artisans. She paused, admiring the intricate woodwork and vibrant textiles, a small smile playing on her lips as she recognized the dedication and skill poured into each piece. Her fingers traced the grain of a beautifully carved jewelry box, and for a moment, she felt a connection to the unknown creator, understanding the love and care that went into their work.

Boaz had been observing the event from a distance, his keen eyes taking in the interactions and dynamics of the community he held so dear. As his gaze settled on Ruth, he found himself inexplicably drawn to her quiet presence. There was something about the way she carried herself, with a grace that spoke of resilience and a gentleness that hinted at a compassionate heart. He watched as she engaged with the artisans' work, noting the genuine appreciation and respect she showed for their efforts.

Intrigued, Boaz approached Ruth, his voice warm and inviting. "I couldn't help but notice your admiration for these pieces. It's refreshing to see someone who truly appreciates the work of our local artisans."

Startled, Ruth turned to face him, her green eyes widening slightly as she took in his confident stance and kind expression. "Oh, yes," she replied softly, a faint blush coloring her cheeks. "There's something so beautiful about the dedication and love that goes into creating something by hand. It's a testament to the human spirit, don't you think?"

Boaz smiled, nodding in agreement. "Absolutely. It's what I strive for in my own business—to create something that not only serves a purpose but also reflects the values and integrity of our community."

As they spoke, Ruth found herself drawn to Boaz's passion and sincerity. His words resonated with her own beliefs, and she felt a kinship in their shared appreciation for hard work and commitment. The conversation flowed effortlessly, their laughter mingling with the chatter of the event.

Yet beneath the easy rapport, Ruth couldn't shake the feeling that there was more to Boaz than met the eye. She sensed a depth and complexity in him, a hint of a story waiting to be told. As the evening wore on and they parted ways, Ruth found her thoughts continually drifting back to the enigmatic man who had so effortlessly captured her attention.

In the days that followed, Ruth found herself thinking about Boaz more often than she cared to admit. His presence had left an indelible mark on her, and she couldn't help but feel drawn to his warmth and authenticity. As she went about her daily tasks, her mind wandered to their conversation, replaying the moments they had shared.

One afternoon, as Ruth sat with Naomi in the cozy kitchen of their shared home, she finally mustered the courage to ask about him. "Naomi," she began tentatively, her fingers tracing the delicate pattern of the teacup in her hands, "what do you know about Boaz Mitchell?"

Naomi's eyes softened, a knowing smile playing at the corners of her lips. "Ah, Boaz," she said, her voice tinged with both admiration and a hint of sadness. "He's a good man, Ruth. One of the best I've ever known."

Ruth leaned forward, her curiosity piqued. "I've heard whispers about him in town, but I don't know much beyond what I've seen myself."

Naomi sighed, settling back into her chair. "Boaz has a heart of gold, but life hasn't always been kind to him. He's faced his share of struggles and heartbreak." She paused, as if weighing her words carefully. "His wife passed away several years ago, leaving him to raise their young son alone. It nearly broke him, but he never lost his faith or his compassion."

Ruth's heart ached for Boaz, imagining the

pain he must have endured. "I had no idea," she whispered, her eyes glistening with empathy.

"He's devoted himself to his family and his community ever since," Naomi continued. "He's always there to lend a helping hand, no matter the cost to himself. People admire him for his strength and kindness, but few truly understand the depth of his sacrifice."

As Naomi spoke, Ruth found herself drawn even more to Boaz. His resilience and selflessness resonated with her own experiences, and she felt a profound connection to his story. She longed to know more about him, to offer comfort and support in whatever way she could.

Lost in thought, Ruth gazed out the window at the golden afternoon light filtering through the trees. She couldn't help but wonder what the future might hold, and whether their paths would continue to intertwine. In that moment, she felt a flicker of hope, a whisper of possibility that perhaps, in each other, they might find the healing and love they both so deeply deserved.

CHAPTER 6

Ruth walked alongside Boaz, the fresh morning dew clinging to her sandals as they made their way through the community garden. The warm rays of the rising sun cast a golden glow across the rows of vegetables, a gentle breeze carrying the scent of herbs and promise. Boaz's voice, deep and reassuring, broke through her reverie as he explained his vision for expanding the garden to include a section dedicated to medicinal plants.

"I believe this could make a real difference in people's lives," he said, his brown eyes alight with passion. "Imagine being able to provide natural remedies to those who might not otherwise have access."

Ruth nodded, her mind already racing with

ideas. "We could host workshops to teach people how to grow and use the plants themselves. Empower them to take control of their own well-being."

A smile spread across Boaz's face, and he turned to her, his gaze filled with admiration. "That's a wonderful idea, Ruth. Your perspective is invaluable."

As they continued to walk, discussing logistics and potential partnerships, Ruth couldn't help but marvel at the man beside her. His dedication to the community, his willingness to invest his time and resources into projects that uplifted others—it was a rare and beautiful thing. She felt a warmth blossoming in her chest, a sense of purpose and belonging that had eluded her for so long.

Boaz paused, kneeling to examine a young tomato plant. His large hands, roughened by years of hard work, gently cradled the delicate leaves. Ruth watched, transfixed by the tenderness of his touch, the reverence with which he tended to the tiny seedling.

"Life is resilient," he murmured, almost to himself. "Even in the face of adversity, it finds a way to grow, to thrive." He glanced up at her then, his eyes searching her face. "You have that same strength within you, Ruth. I see it in the way you care for others, in the way you've embraced this community as your own."

Ruth felt her cheeks flush, a flutter of something unnamed stirring in her heart. She looked away, her gaze settling on the distant hills, their peaks shrouded in morning mist. How long had it been since someone had seen her, truly seen her, beyond the mask of grief and uncertainty she wore? In Boaz's presence, she felt seen, understood in a way that both thrilled and terrified her.

They worked side by side in comfortable silence, hands brushing occasionally as they reached for tools or seedlings. As the sun climbed higher in the sky, Ruth found herself stealing glances at Boaz, admiring the strong lines of his profile, the gentleness of his smile. In the golden light of morning, amid the rich earth and burgeoning life, something new and fragile took root in her heart—a tender shoot of hope, a whisper of possibility.

Naomi's weathered hands wrapped around a steaming mug of tea, her keen eyes studying Ruth's pensive expression. "You seem lost in thought, my dear," she remarked gently, a knowing smile tugging at the corners of her mouth. "Could it be that a certain someone has captured your attention?"

Ruth startled, nearly spilling her own tea as she met Naomi's gaze. "I don't know what you mean," she demurred, but the telltale blush creeping up her neck betrayed her words. She fidgeted with the hem of her modest skirt, suddenly finding the worn fabric utterly fascinating.

"Oh, come now," Naomi chuckled, reaching across the table to pat Ruth's hand. "I've seen the way Boaz looks at you, the way his eyes light up when you're near. And you, my dear, seem to come alive in his presence."

Ruth shook her head, a wistful sigh escaping her lips. "It's not like that, Naomi. Boaz is a kind and generous man, but he could never see me as more than a friend, a fellow member of the community." She traced the rim of her mug with a fingertip, her thoughts drifting to the quiet moments they'd shared, the unspoken connection that seemed to grow with each passing day.

Naomi leaned back in her chair, her gaze softening with understanding. "You underestimate yourself, Ruth. Your strength, your compassion, your resilience—these are qualities that any man would be fortunate to have by his side." She paused, her voice dropping to a conspiratorial whisper. "And if I'm not mistaken, Boaz has already begun to recognize the treasure that you are."

Ruth's heart skipped a beat, a fragile hope unfurling within her chest. Could it be true? Could Boaz, with his steadfast faith and unwavering integrity, truly see her as more than a broken woman seeking solace in a new life? She closed her eyes, remembering the warmth of his smile, the gentleness of his touch as they worked side by side in the community garden.

And yet, the wounds of her past still ached, the memory of love lost casting a shadow over the possibility of a future. "I don't know if I'm ready," she whispered, her voice trembling with emotion. "What if I open my heart again, only to have it shattered once more?"

Naomi's eyes glistened with unshed tears, her own grief a palpable presence in the room. "My child, love is always a risk. But it is also a gift, a precious thing to be cherished and nurtured." She reached out, cupping Ruth's face with a tender hand. "Don't let fear rob you of the beauty that may lie ahead. Trust in God's plan, and trust in the goodness of your own heart."

Ruth leaned into Naomi's touch, drawing strength from the older woman's wisdom and compassion. Perhaps, she mused, it was time to step out in faith, to allow herself the possibility of a future filled with love and partnership. Perhaps, in Boaz's steadfast presence, she would find the healing and wholeness she so desperately craved.

CHAPTER 7

Ruth's fingers intertwined with the tall grass as she walked beside Boaz through the sun-dappled meadow, the afternoon light casting a golden glow over their path. The scent of wildflowers wafted on the gentle breeze, encircling them in a sweet embrace. She glanced over at Boaz, admiring his strong profile and the way his eyes crinkled at the corners when he smiled.

"I'm glad we could finally spend some time together outside of work," Boaz said, his voice warm and resonant. "I've been meaning to ask you more about your background, Ruth. What brought you to our little town?"

Ruth took a deep breath, considering her words carefully. Memories of her late husband flickered through her mind like the shadows of birds in flight, here one moment and gone the next. "After my husband passed away, I felt adrift in the city, like a leaf torn from its branch. My mother-in-law Naomi suggested we move here for a fresh start, to surround ourselves with a supportive community."

Boaz nodded, his gaze filled with empathy. "I'm so sorry for your loss, Ruth. Starting over in a new place takes tremendous courage."

"Thank you, Boaz. It hasn't been easy, but I'm learning to find strength in my faith and the kindness of others." She smiled softly, appreciating his genuine concern.

As they continued their stroll, the conversation turned to shared values and experiences. Ruth discovered that Boaz's commitment to sustainability and community mirrored her own passions. She had always admired his innovative approach to business, but now she saw the depth of his character shining through.

"Running the grocery stores has been both rewarding and challenging," Boaz confided, his brow furrowing slightly. "Sometimes I worry that I'm not doing enough to support our local farmers and artisans, or that I'm neglecting my own well-being in the process."

Ruth placed a comforting hand on his arm, her touch light yet reassuring. "From what I've seen, you're making a real difference in people's lives, Boaz. Your dedication is inspiring, but it's important to take care of yourself too."

He smiled gratefully, his hand briefly covering hers in a gesture of appreciation. "Thank you, Ruth. Your perspective means a lot to me."

As the sun began to dip towards the horizon, painting the sky in shades of amber and rose, Ruth and Boaz found themselves drawn into a comfortable silence. The unspoken connection between them grew, nurtured by the sharing of their stories and the understanding that blossomed in the space between their words.

Walking side by side, their hearts beat in sync with the gentle rhythm of the breeze, and for a moment, the weight of their pasts seemed to lift, replaced by the promise of a future where hope and love could take root and flourish.

As they continued their walk, Ruth and Boaz found themselves at the edge of a small pond, its surface shimmering with the reflection of the setting sun. They paused, taking in the tranquil beauty of the scene before them, each lost in their own thoughts.

Ruth's gaze drifted to a pair of swans gliding gracefully across the water, their movements perfectly synchronized. She marveled at the way they seemed to intuitively understand one another, their bond unspoken yet undeniable. In that moment, she felt a flutter in her heart, a whisper of something she hadn't dared to hope for since her husband's passing.

Boaz, too, found himself captivated by the swans, their effortless unity stirring a longing within him. He glanced at Ruth, her profile illuminated by the golden light, and he was struck by the realization that she had become more than just a friend to him. In her, he saw a kindred spirit, someone who understood the joys and sorrows of life, and who faced each day with a quiet strength that inspired him.

As if sensing his gaze, Ruth turned to meet his eyes, and in that shared glance, a world of unspoken emotions passed between them. Her green eyes, usually guarded, now held a softness that took his breath away, and he felt himself drawn to her in a way he had never experienced before.

Slowly, tentatively, Boaz reached out and brushed a stray lock of hair from Ruth's face, his fingers lingering for a moment on her cheek. She leaned into his touch, her eyes fluttering closed as a sigh escaped her lips.

In that instant, the world around them faded away, and all that existed was the connection between two souls who had found solace and understanding in each other. It was a moment of profound intimacy, not of the body, but of the heart, a recognition of the love that had taken root and begun to blossom.

And as they stood there, bathed in the golden light of the setting sun, Ruth and Boaz knew that their lives had been forever changed, their paths now intertwined by a bond that could weather any storm.

CHAPTER 8

R uth felt the disapproving stares of the church ladies pierce the back of her neck like hot needles as she walked hand-in-hand with Boaz down the center aisle. Their whispered judgment hissed in her ears - "gold digger," "fallen woman," "using that kind man." Ruth held her head high, refusing to let their narrow minds and cold hearts dim the warmth blooming inside her whenever Boaz's hand enveloped hers.

Still, doubt gnawed at the edges of her burgeoning hope. What could a successful, respected man like Boaz see in a struggling widow from the wrong side of the tracks? Perhaps they were right about her...

Boaz glanced over at Ruth, concern etching lines between his eyebrows as he sensed her unease. He squeezed her hand reassuringly, drawing her nearer to his side as if shielding her from their scathing opprobrium with his sturdy frame. Ruth sent him a small, grateful smile, but inside her stomach churned. She couldn't bear it if their disapproval and gossip caused problems for Boaz, the man who'd become her shelter in the storm.

Outside the chapel, Boaz's second-in-command at the store approached with harried steps. "Sir, I'm sorry to bother you on a Sunday, but we have a situation with a supplier that needs your immediate attention." Duty and desire warred on Boaz's face as he glanced from his employee to Ruth.

"Go," Ruth murmured, masking her disappointment. "Your business needs you. I understand." Hadn't it always been this way? Everyone needed a piece of this giving man. Who was she to demand more than he could spare?

Boaz captured her chin gently, tilting it up to meet his sincere gaze. "I'll take care of this as quickly as I can. But know this, Ruth. You're important to me. More than you realize." His eyes held an unspoken promise that made her pulse trip and a bittersweet ache swell beneath her breastbone.

With obvious reluctance, Boaz released her and strode away, his broad shoulders carrying the weight of myriad responsibilities. Ruth watched him go, wrapping her arms around herself as if to hold in the lingering warmth of his touch. Would there ever be a time when she didn't feel like an afterthought, caught between his sense of obligation to business and family? She ducked her head as she walked to her car alone, doubts and insecurities whispering through her mind like an insidious breeze.

Ruth's steps felt laden as she trudged up the walkway to the modest home she shared with Naomi. The scent of honeysuckle lingered in the air, but its usual sweetness tasted bitter on her tongue. She paused at the door, her hand resting on the weathered wood, steeling herself to conceal the turmoil churning within.

Inside, Naomi sat in her favorite armchair, a patchwork quilt draped across her lap. Her eyes, wise and knowing, immediately sought Ruth's as she entered. "What troubles you, my daughter?" The gentleness in her voice, the genuine concern etched into the lines of her face, broke through Ruth's fragile composure.

Tears blurred her vision as she sank onto the sofa, her voice trembling. "Am I fooling myself, Naomi? Boaz... his life is so full, his responsibilities so great. What can I offer him? I'm just..." She gestured helplessly, the words sticking in her throat.

Naomi reached out, clasping Ruth's hands in her own work-worn ones. "Just what? A woman of strength? Of compassion? Of unwavering faith?" Naomi's eyes shone with fierce love. "Ruth, you are a treasure. Never doubt your worth."

Ruth shook her head, a rueful smile tugging at her lips despite the ache in her chest. "But his business, his family... they'll always come first."

"My child, you have weathered storms that would break lesser souls. Trust in the path the Lord has set before you." Naomi's fingers tightened around Ruth's. "And trust in Boaz. His heart is true, his character unshakable. The seeds of love you've sown together will bear fruit in due time."

Ruth leaned into Naomi's strength, absorbing her words like parched earth soaking in rain. The knots in her stomach began to loosen, replaced by a tentative unfurling of hope. Perhaps she needed to have faith, not just in a higher power, but in the man who had shown her such unwavering kindness and respect.

Drawing a deep breath, Ruth straightened her spine, a new resolve settling over her. She would hold fast to her own truth, to the quiet resilience that had carried her this far. And she would trust that Boaz's steadfast nature would guide him back to her, no matter the challenges that lay ahead.

As if sensing the shift in her demeanor, Naomi smiled, her eyes crinkling at the corners. "There's my strong girl." She patted Ruth's cheek affectionately. "Now, let's put on some tea and you can tell me all about your day. The good Lord knows we could both use a bit of everyday chatter to soothe the soul."

Ruth smiled, a genuine curve of her lips this time. With Naomi's wisdom to steady her and the budding promise of Boaz's affection, she could face whatever trials lay ahead. For now, she would steep herself in the comfort of family and faith, trusting that love would find a way to flourish amidst life's thorny paths.

CHAPTER 9

The golden light of dawn seeped through the windows of the community center, illuminating the worried faces huddled inside. Ruth stood among them, her chestnut hair swept back in a loose bun, her eyes filled with quiet determination. She listened intently as the town elders discussed the crisis at hand—a sudden shortage of essential supplies due to a delivery truck breakdown on the highway leading into town.

Ruth stepped forward, her voice soft but clear. "I may be new here, but I believe I can help. In my previous job, I coordinated logistics for a mid-sized company. If you'll allow me, I can reach out to my contacts and see if we can arrange an emergency delivery."

The elders exchanged glances, their expressions a mix of surprise and hesitation. Boaz, standing at the edge of the group, caught Ruth's eye and gave her an encouraging nod. His warmth gave her the confidence to continue. "I know it's a lot to ask, but I want to do my part for this community that has welcomed me so graciously."

After a moment of deliberation, the elders agreed to let Ruth take the lead. She dove into action, making phone calls and sending emails, her fingers flying across her laptop keyboard. Hours passed as she worked tirelessly, fueled by a desire to prove her worth and help those in need.

As the sun began to set, a delivery truck rumbled into town, its cargo hold filled with the much-needed supplies. The community members cheered, their faces alight with relief and gratitude. Ruth stood back, a small smile playing on her lips, feeling a sense of accomplishment and belonging.

Boaz approached her, his brown eyes warm with admiration. "You did an incredible thing today, Ruth. The town is lucky to have you."

She ducked her head, a blush creeping up her cheeks. "I just wanted to help. This community has given me so much already."

"You've given us even more," Boaz said softly.

He reached out and squeezed her hand, a gesture of support and understanding. In that moment, Ruth felt a flicker of something more—a connection that went beyond gratitude and respect.

As the townspeople began unloading the supplies, Ruth and Boaz worked side by side, their hands brushing occasionally as they passed boxes back and forth. A silent understanding passed between them, a recognition of the challenges they had faced and the strength they had found in each other.

Ruth knew that her journey in this new town was far from over, but with Boaz by her side and the support of the community, she felt ready to face whatever lay ahead. She had proven her worth, not just to others but to herself, and that knowledge filled her with a quiet sense of pride and purpose.

As the day drew to a close and the last of the supplies were distributed, Ruth and Boaz found themselves lingering in the town square, reluctant to part ways. The golden hues of the setting sun bathed the scene in a warm glow, casting long shadows across the cobblestone streets. Ruth's chestnut hair shimmered in the fading light, and Boaz couldn't help but admire the way it framed her delicate features.

"Thank you for everything today," Ruth said, her voice soft and sincere. "I couldn't have done it without your support."

Boaz shook his head, a gentle smile tugging at the corners of his mouth. "You underestimate yourself, Ruth. Your strength and compassion are what made the difference."

They stood in comfortable silence for a moment, each lost in their own thoughts. Ruth's mind drifted to the challenges that lay ahead—the uncertainty of her future, the weight of her past, and the growing feelings she had for the man standing beside her. She knew that their relationship was complicated, fraught with obstacles and expectations, but in that moment, none of it seemed to matter.

Boaz, too, felt the pull of their connection, the unspoken bond that had formed between them. He had watched Ruth blossom in the face of adversity, her quiet determination and unwavering faith inspiring him in ways he had never expected. He knew that their path forward would not be easy, but he also knew that he would stand by her side, no matter what.

As if reading each other's thoughts, they turned to face one another, their eyes locking in a gaze that spoke volumes. In that silent exchange, a decision was made—a choice to move forward together, to face the challenges that lay ahead as partners, as equals, as two hearts intertwined by fate and circumstance.

Ruth reached out, her hand finding Boaz's, their fingers interlacing in a gesture of unity and trust. The warmth of his touch spread through her, a comforting reminder of the strength she had found in him. Together, they walked through the town square, their steps falling into a natural rhythm, a symbol of the journey they had embarked upon, side by side, heart to heart.

CHAPTER 10

oaz walked through the rows of his organic grocery store, his mind preoccupied with thoughts of Ruth. He paused by a display of fresh herbs, their fragrant scents wafting up to greet him. Rosemary, thyme, basil—the herbs they had planted together in the community garden just last week. A smile played at the corners of his mouth as he recalled Ruth's laughter, the way the sunlight had caught her hair as she knelt in the rich soil.

His fingers brushed against the delicate leaves, an idea taking shape. He would propose to her in the garden, surrounded by the fruits of their shared labor. A symbol of the life they could build together, rooted in faith, love, and partnership.

Boaz spent the next few days planning, his heart full of anticipation. He selected a simple but elegant ring, a band of gold entwined with a single diamond, like two lives intertwined as one.

When the moment arrived, Boaz led Ruth to the garden at dusk, the golden hour casting a warm glow over the plants they had nurtured. Ruth looked radiant in the fading light, her eyes shining with curiosity.

"Ruth," Boaz began, taking her hands in his. "When I'm with you, I feel the Lord's presence more deeply than I ever have before. Your faith, your resilience, your gentle spirit—they inspire me every day."

He dropped to one knee, pulling the ring from his pocket. Ruth's hand flew to her mouth, her eyes widening.

"I want to walk beside you for all my days, in service to God and to each other. Ruth, will you marry me?"

Tears glistened in Ruth's eyes as she pulled Boaz to his feet and into an embrace. "Yes," she whispered against his shoulder. "Yes, with all my heart."

They held each other as the sun dipped below the horizon, bathing the garden in a soft, ethereal light. A new beginning and a testament to the power of love and the grace of God.

Ruth pulled back, her eyes searching Boaz's face, a kaleidoscope of emotions playing across her delicate features. Joy, relief, and a hint of disbelief mingled in her expression as she processed the momentous shift in her life's trajectory. Her thoughts drifted to her late husband, the love they had shared, and the grief that had consumed her in the wake of his passing. She had never imagined that her heart could open itself to love again, yet here she stood, in the arms of a man who had shown her unwavering kindness and devotion.

"I never thought I'd find love again," Ruth confessed, her voice barely above a whisper. "After everything I've been through, I feared my heart would remain closed forever."

Boaz gently cupped her face, his thumb brushing away a stray tear. "Your capacity for love is one of the many things I admire about you, Ruth. Your heart has endured so much, yet it still overflows with compassion and grace."

Ruth leaned into his touch, a soft smile gracing her lips. "It's because of you, Boaz. Your steadfast presence and unwavering faith have helped me heal in ways I never thought possible."

As they stood together in the garden, the newly engaged couple basked in the serenity of the moment. The gentle breeze carried the sweet fragrance of the blooming flowers, a symbol of the new life they were about to embark upon together. Ruth knew that her journey had been one of loss and redemption, but standing here with Boaz, she felt a renewed sense of purpose and belonging.

"I can't wait to start this new chapter with you," Ruth said, her eyes shining with anticipation. "To build a life together, rooted in faith and love."

Boaz smiled, his heart full of gratitude for the incredible woman before him. "Together, we'll face whatever the future holds, always trusting in God's plan for us."

He leaned in and kissed her lips for the first time. It was a sweet and tender kiss filled with promise and their shared faith.

As the last rays of sunlight faded, Ruth and Boaz walked hand in hand back to the house, ready to share their joyous news with Naomi and the rest of their community. For Ruth, this moment marked a turning point, a testament to the resilience of the human spirit and the transformative power of love in the face of adversity.

CHAPTER 11

Naomi stepped into the sun-dappled chapel, the familiar scent of polished wood and stone enveloping her. Memories flooded back as she took a seat in the worn pew, the grain of the oak smooth beneath her weathered hands. The face of her late husband Samuel flickered in her mind, an apparition from a life that now seemed distant, like a half-remembered dream.

As the organ music swelled, Naomi closed her eyes, allowing the melodic notes to wash over her. Tears pricked at the corners of her eyes. She had avoided this place for so long after Samuel's passing, the pain too raw, the void too vast. But now, in the stillness of the chapel, she felt a glimmer of something she had thought lost forever—peace.

Reverend Josiah's rich baritone voice filled the

space as he began the sermon, speaking of hope in times of sorrow, of light in the darkness. Naomi's heart stirred with each word, a flicker of renewal kindling within her soul. As the congregation rose to sing a hymn, she found herself joining in, her voice tentative at first but growing stronger with each verse.

After the service concluded, Naomi lingered, her gaze wandering over the stained glass windows that cast a kaleidoscope of colors across the stone floor. Reverend Josiah approached, his kind eyes crinkling at the corners as he smiled. "Naomi, it's wonderful to see you here. How have you been holding up?"

She met his gaze, surprised to find her voice steady. "Taking it one day at a time, Reverend. It's been...challenging, but I'm learning to find my way again."

He nodded, his hand coming to rest on her shoulder in a comforting gesture. "The path of grief is never easy, but remember, you are not alone. The community is here for you, always."

Naomi felt a lump form in her throat, touched by the sincerity in his words. "Thank you, Reverend. That means more than you know."

As she made her way out of the chapel, Naomi

felt a lightness in her step that she hadn't experienced in months. Perhaps, in this close-knit community, she could find not only solace but also a renewed sense of belonging.

Later that evening, Naomi and Ruth sat together on the porch swing, sipping tea as the sun dipped below the horizon, painting the sky in hues of orange and pink. A comfortable silence stretched between them, broken only by the gentle creaking of the swing.

Ruth's voice was soft when she finally spoke. "I've been thinking about how much has changed since we left the city. It hasn't been easy, but I'm grateful we made this journey together."

Naomi reached over, clasping her daughter-in-law's hand in her own. "As am I, Ruth. Your strength and compassion have been a beacon of light for me in some of my darkest moments."

"We've both had to be strong," Ruth mused, her gaze distant. "Leaving behind everything we knew, starting over in a new place. It's taken courage."

"And faith," Naomi added, a small smile tugging at her lips. "Faith in each other, in the path we've chosen, and in the belief that better days lie ahead."

As the last rays of sunlight faded, Naomi and Ruth remained on the porch, their hands entwined, each drawing strength from the other. They had weathered storms together, and now, in the stillness of the evening, they could feel the promise of a brighter tomorrow on the horizon.

———

The gentle chime of wedding bells echoed through the small chapel, the sound reverberating off the whitewashed walls and filling the air with a sense of joyous celebration. Ruth stood before the altar, her hand intertwined with Boaz's, their eyes locked in a gaze that spoke volumes of the love and devotion they shared. The lace of her simple, elegant gown brushed against her skin as she turned to face her husband, a soft smile playing on her lips.

"I now pronounce you husband and wife," the pastor declared, his voice warm and filled with genuine happiness for the couple. "You may kiss the bride."

Boaz's strong hands cupped Ruth's face as he leaned in, their lips meeting in a tender, heartfelt kiss that sealed their union. In that moment, the world seemed to fall away, leaving only the two of them, their hearts beating as one.

As they turned to face their gathered friends and family, Ruth's eyes sought out Naomi, who sat in the front row, tears of joy glistening on her cheeks. The older woman's face was alight with pride and love for her daughter-in-law, and Ruth felt a surge of gratitude for the unwavering support Naomi had shown her throughout their journey.

Hand in hand, Ruth and Boaz made their way down the aisle, the soft petals of rose and lavender raining down upon them as they stepped out into the warm sunlight. The future stretched before them, filled with promise and possibility, and Ruth knew that with Boaz by her side and Naomi as an integral part of their family, they could face whatever challenges lay ahead.

In the days that followed, Ruth and Boaz began to build their new life together, their love serving as the foundation upon which they would create a home filled with warmth, laughter, and unconditional support. Naomi's presence was a constant comfort, her wisdom and guidance invaluable as the young couple navigated the joys and challenges of married life.

As Ruth settled into her new role as a wife, she found herself reflecting on the winding path that had led her to this moment. The pain of loss, the uncertainty of starting anew, and the courage it had taken to open her heart once more—all of these experiences had shaped her, molding her into the woman she was today. And now, with Boaz's love and Naomi's unwavering support, she knew that she had finally found her place in the world, a sense of belonging that filled her with a profound peace.

In the quiet moments, when she watched Boaz and Naomi laughing together over a shared meal or working side by side in the garden, Ruth's heart swelled with a love so fierce and pure that it took her breath away. This, she knew, was the true meaning of family—a bond that transcended blood, forged in the fires of shared experience and strengthened by the power of unconditional love.

CHAPTER 12

Ruth's eyes traced the lines of Boaz's strong hands as they cradled the delicate teacup. Steam rose in gentle wisps, mirroring the unfurling of her own heart in his presence. They sat in the cozy nook of his office above the organic grocery store, a space that had become their sanctuary amidst the bustle of the town below.

"I've been thinking," Boaz began, his voice a soothing rumble, "about how we might weave our lives together more fully. Not just in our hearts, but in our day-to-day."

Ruth met his gaze, a flicker of anticipation dancing in her emerald eyes. "Tell me more," she encouraged softly, leaning forward.

His smile was warm, encompassing. "You have such a gift for connecting with people, Ruth. The way you listen, the empathy you exude. I've seen it in how you interact with our customers, our community." He paused, considering. "What if we created a role for you here? A community liaison of sorts, helping to strengthen the bonds between our store and the people we serve."

The idea bloomed in Ruth's mind, a seed taking root in fertile soil. It was an opportunity to blend her past experience in marketing with her innate desire to make a difference. To build something meaningful alongside the man she loved.

"Boaz," she breathed, reaching for his hand, "that sounds wonderful. A way to use my skills and passions to give back to this place that has become our home."

He threaded his fingers through hers, a perfect fit. "Together, I believe we can create something truly special. Not just for us, but for everyone here."

Ruth's mind drifted to the possibilities - partnering with local schools, organizing community events, finding ways to support those in need. It was a vision of a future rich with purpose and connection.

As they continued to discuss ideas, their excitement grew, filling the space between them with a palpable energy. In that moment, Ruth felt a deep sense of belonging. Not just to Boaz, but to this path they were forging side by side.

Their conversation flowed easily, punctuated by laughter and the occasional comfortable silence. Through the window, Ruth could see the town square, alive with activity. Children playing, neighbors chatting, a vibrant tapestry of life.

And she knew, with a certainty that settled deep in her bones, that this was where she was meant to be. That together, she and Boaz would continue to nurture this community, to help it flourish and grow.

It was a love story, yes. But it was also a story of resilience, of hope, of the transformative power of connection. As Ruth leaned into Boaz's embrace, she felt the pieces of her life falling into place, forming a mosaic of grace and purpose.

In that small office, perched above the beating heart of their town, Ruth and Boaz began to write the next chapter of their journey. A chapter filled with love, with service, with the quiet joy of building a life rooted in faith and community. And as the sun dipped low on the horizon, casting the room in a warm, golden glow, they knew that this was just the beginning.

Naomi sat in her favorite armchair, a well-worn quilt draped across her lap. She gazed out the window, watching as the sun began its slow descent, painting the sky in hues of orange and pink. The gentle hum of conversation drifted from the kitchen, where Ruth and Boaz were preparing dinner together, their laughter mingling with the clatter of pots and pans.

A smile tugged at the corners of Naomi's lips, a sense of contentment settling deep within her heart. It had been a long and winding road, marked by grief and uncertainty. But now, as she listened to the joyful sounds of her daughter-in-law and the man who had become like a son to her, Naomi knew that they had finally found their way home.

She closed her eyes, allowing the warmth of the moment to wash over her. In her mind's eye, she could see the future stretching out before them, a tapestry woven with threads of love, faith, and community. She could picture the children that Ruth and Boaz would raise together, their laughter echoing through the halls of their home. She could envision the ways in which they would continue to serve their town, their love for one another spilling out and touching the lives of all those around them.

Naomi's thoughts were interrupted by the gentle touch of Ruth's hand on her shoulder. She opened her eyes to find her daughter-in-law smiling down at her, her eyes shining with a joy that Naomi had once feared she might never see again.

"Dinner's ready," Ruth said softly, her voice filled with warmth. "Come join us, Mother."

Naomi nodded, allowing Ruth to help her to her feet. As they made their way to the kitchen, Naomi's heart swelled with gratitude for the blessings that had been bestowed upon their family. The road had been long, but it had led them to this moment, to this place of love and belonging.

As they gathered around the table, hands clasped in prayer, Naomi knew that this was just the beginning of a beautiful new chapter. A chapter filled with the love of family, the strength of faith, and the enduring power of hope. And as she looked into the faces of Ruth and Boaz, she saw reflected back at her a love that would stand the test of time, a love that would be a beacon of light for all the days to come.

CHAPTER 13

The golden sun warmed Ruth's face as she stood in the whispering wheat fields, their gentle swaying like a symphony of nature's grace. Her heart swelled with gratitude, marveling at the twists of fate that had brought her to this moment—a crossroads where sorrow and hope intertwined.

She thought of her beloved husband, taken too soon, and the ache that still resided within. Yet amidst the pain, she had found an unexpected anchor in Naomi, her mother-in-law, whose strength and faith had been a guiding light in the darkness. Together they had journeyed to this quiet hamlet, seeking solace and perhaps a chance to begin anew.

And then there was Boaz, her new husband. His kindness had been a balm to her weary soul from the moment they met. In his presence, she felt seen, understood in a way that transcended mere words. His gentle smile and the warmth of his gaze spoke volumes, offering comfort and love—something she thought she would never have again.

Ruth closed her eyes, breathing in the earthy scent of the fields. The loyalty and love she had known, though tinged with grief, had taught her the true meaning of devotion. And now, in this small community that had embraced her, she sensed the stirrings of a second chance—an opportunity to open her heart once more.

Nearby, Boaz walked among the bustling workers, offering words of encouragement and gratitude. Yet his thoughts were never far from Ruth. Her quiet strength and compassion had touched something deep within him, awakening emotions he had long thought dormant.

He marveled at the way she had seamlessly woven herself into the fabric of their community, her presence a catalyst for change. The once reserved townsfolk now greeted each other with warm smiles, their hearts lightened by her gentle spirit. Even his own staff seemed more engaged, their work infused with a newfound sense of purpose.

As he watched Ruth in the distance, her figure bathed in the golden light, Boaz felt a sudden clarity wash over him. Together, they were stronger —not just as individuals, but as a force for good in this small corner of the world. With her by his side, he knew they could weather any storm, their love a beacon of hope for all who crossed their path.

The joyous laughter of children filled the air, their innocent faces aglow with delight as they danced around the newlyweds. Ruth and Boaz, hand in hand, moved through the gathered crowd, their steps light and their smiles radiant. The entire community had come together to celebrate their union, a testament to the profound impact the couple had made on their lives.

Naomi watched from the sidelines, her weathered face etched with a mixture of joy and bittersweet remembrance. In Ruth, she saw the echoes of her own beloved daughter-in-law, whose unwavering loyalty had been a balm to her grieving soul. Now, as Ruth embarked on this new chapter, Naomi felt a sense of peace wash over her, knowing that her son's memory would live on through the love that Ruth and Boaz shared.

As the couple reached the center of the gathering, Boaz turned to face Ruth, his eyes shimmering with emotion. "My beloved," he whispered, his voice thick with feeling, "you have brought light into my life and the lives of all those around us. Your compassion and strength have transformed this community, and I am forever grateful to have you by my side."

Ruth gazed up at him, her heart swelling with love and gratitude. "Boaz, my love," she replied softly, "it is through your unwavering support and the kindness of this community that I have found my home. Together, we will continue to nurture and uplift those around us, just as they have done for me."

As the couple embraced, the crowd erupted in cheers and applause, their voices rising in a joyful chorus. The air hummed with a sense of unity and purpose, a testament to the power of love to heal and transform even the most wounded of hearts.

And as the celebration continued late into the

night, Ruth and Boaz knew that their journey was only just beginning. With each other and their beloved community by their side, they would face whatever challenges lay ahead, their love a guiding light in the darkness.

EPILOGUE

The warm breeze gently rustled the wheat fields as the golden late afternoon sun cast long shadows across the land. Ruth's auburn hair shimmered in the fading light as she walked hand-in-hand with Boaz along the edge of the field. They savored the peaceful moment, hearts full of gratitude for the journey that had brought them together.

Boaz slowed his pace and turned to face Ruth, his brown eyes filled with affection. "Can you believe it's been a year since we first met?" His voice was soft, almost reverent.

"It feels like a lifetime ago," Ruth replied, her gaze locked with his. The hardships and uncertainties of the past seemed distant now, replaced by a deep sense of belonging and purpose. She squeezed his hand gently, conveying the depth of her emotions without words.

Perhaps this is what true happiness feels like, Ruth mused inwardly. *Not the fleeting joy of a moment, but the steady warmth of a love that has weathered storms and grown stronger.*

They continued their leisurely stroll, the rustling of the wheat stalks a soothing symphony. Ruth's mind wandered to the challenges they had faced—the initial hesitation from some in the community, the long hours spent working side-by-side to make their dreams a reality. Yet through it all, their bond had only deepened, rooted in a shared faith and unwavering commitment to each other.

As they neared the old oak tree at the edge of the property, Boaz paused once more. He reached out to tuck a stray lock of hair behind Ruth's ear, his touch tender and familiar. "I thank God every day for bringing you into my life," he murmured. "You've taught me so much about resilience, about trusting in His plan even when the path isn't clear."

Ruth leaned into his touch, a soft smile playing on her lips. "And you've shown me the true meaning of steadfast love and support. I couldn't imagine this journey without you by my side."

From the porch of the nearby farmhouse, Naomi watched the couple, her heart swelling with contentment. The years of grief and uncertainty had given way to a peace she had never thought possible. *My sweet Ruth, you've found your home at last*, she thought, her eyes misting with a mixture of joy and nostalgia.

Naomi's gaze drifted to the vibrant garden she had been tending, a tangible reminder of the new life that had taken root in their hearts. She knew that there would still be challenges ahead, but with the love and support of their little family, they could weather any storm.

As the sun dipped below the horizon, painting the sky in hues of orange and pink, Ruth and Boaz made their way back to the farmhouse, their laughter floating on the evening breeze. Naomi smiled, offering a silent prayer of thanks for the blessings that had brought them to this moment—a testament to the enduring power of faith, love, and the unbreakable bonds of family.

Later, Ruth stood at the edge of the field alone, her fingers grazing the golden stalks of wheat as they swayed in the gentle breeze. The sun hung low in the sky, casting a warm glow across the landscape and bathing everything in a soft, ethereal light. In this moment of quiet contemplation, Ruth felt a profound sense of gratitude wash over her, filling her heart with a peace she had once thought impossible.

How far we've come, she mused, her thoughts drifting to the winding path that had led her to this place. The pain of loss, the uncertainty of starting anew, and the unwavering love and support of those who had become her family—all of these experiences had shaped her, molding her into the woman she was today.

Ruth's mind wandered to Boaz, the man who had shown her the true depth of unconditional love. His steadfast presence had been a beacon of hope in her darkest hours, guiding her through the storms of grief and self-doubt. In his eyes, she had found a reflection of her own strength, a reminder that even in the face of adversity, love could prevail.

As she stood there, surrounded by the fruits of their labor, Ruth couldn't help but marvel at the resilience of the human spirit. The community that had welcomed her with open arms had taught her the true meaning of belonging, of being part of something greater than herself. In their shared joys and sorrows, she had discovered the unbreakable bonds of loyalty and compassion that had the power to transform lives.

A smile played on her lips as she whispered a silent prayer of thanks, her words carried on the wind like a sacred offering. "Thank you, Lord, for the blessings you have bestowed upon us. For the love that has healed our broken hearts, and for the hope that guides us forward."

With a final glance at the golden fields, Ruth turned back towards the farmhouse, her heart filled with the knowledge that no matter what the future held, she would face it with the strength and courage born of an unshakable faith and the love of those who walked beside her.

EXCERPT FROM ESTHER

Esther's heels clicked against the polished marble floor of the sleek office tower as she strode towards the executive conference room, her thoughts a swirling tempest of ambition and apprehension. The weight of responsibility hung heavily upon her shoulders, a mantle she had willingly donned in her ascent through the corporate ranks. Yet, beneath the veneer of professionalism, the echoes of her humble beginnings lingered, a constant reminder of the delicate balance she sought to maintain between her burgeoning career and the unshakable bonds of family.

As she stepped into the conference room, the floor-to-ceiling windows offered a breathtaking panorama of the bustling metropolis below, a veritable labyrinth of hopes and dreams etched in steel and glass. Esther's gaze drifted to the horizon, where the sun's rays danced upon the distant rooftops, casting an ethereal glow that seemed to whisper of untold possibilities. She drew a steadying breath, steeling herself for the challenges that lay ahead, knowing that each decision she made would ripple through the lives of those she held dear.

Across town, in the hallowed halls of City Hall, Mayor Xander Harrison stood before a sea of eager faces, his charismatic presence commanding the attention of all who gathered. His voice, rich with authority and tinged with an undercurrent of empathy, resounded through the crowded chamber as he unveiled his latest initiative.

"My fellow citizens," he began, his piercing blue eyes sweeping over the assembled throng. "Today, we embark upon a journey that will reshape the very fabric of our beloved city. In our search for a new spokesperson, we seek not merely a voice, but a beacon of hope and inspiration. Together, we shall forge a path towards a brighter future, where every voice is heard, and every dream is within reach."

As the mayor's words washed over the captivated audience, a palpable energy surged through the room, igniting a spark of excitement and anticipation. The city's elite, resplendent in their tailored suits and designer gowns, exchanged knowing glances and hushed whispers, each vying for a piece of the limelight that would inevitably follow this momentous declaration.

Esther, lost in thought as she gazed out at the city below, felt a flicker of unease deep within her soul. She couldn't shake the feeling that her carefully constructed world was about to be upended, that the delicate equilibrium she had fought so hard to maintain was teetering on the brink of chaos. And yet, a small voice within her whispered that perhaps this was the very opportunity she had been seeking, a chance to make a difference, to leave an indelible mark upon the tapestry of her beloved city.

With a heavy sigh, Esther turned from the

window, her resolve hardening with each passing moment.

A sharp knock at her office door jolted Esther from her reverie. She smoothed the fabric of her skirt, a subtle armor against the unexpected, and called out, "Come in."

The door swung open, revealing the towering figure of her supervisor, Mr. Jameson. His usually stoic features were alight with an inscrutable emotion as he strode toward her desk, a crisp envelope clutched in his hand.

"Esther," he began, his voice a mix of incredulity and admiration, "I have some news that may come as a surprise to you." He paused, as if searching for the right words. "Mayor Harrison's office has personally requested your participation in the selection process for the new mayoral spokesperson."

The words hung in the air, their weight palpable. Esther's mind raced, trying to comprehend the implications of this unexpected development. She had always prided herself on her dedication to her work, her unwavering commitment to excellence, but this? This was beyond anything she had ever imagined.

"I...I don't know what to say," she managed, her voice barely above a whisper. "Why me?"

Mr. Jameson's lips curved into a wry smile. "Why not you, Esther? You've proven yourself time and again, both in your work and in your character. The mayor's office recognizes that, and they believe you have the potential to be an exceptional spokesperson for our city."

Esther's thoughts turned to her family, to the sacrifices they had made to support her dreams. She thought of the countless hours she had spent honing her skills, pushing herself to be better, to make a difference. And now, here was an opportunity to do just that, to step onto a larger stage and be a voice for change.

But even as excitement coursed through her veins, Esther couldn't shake the nagging doubts that crept into the corners of her mind. Was she truly ready for such a monumental responsibility? Could she bear the weight of an entire city's hopes and dreams upon her shoulders?

As if sensing her inner turmoil, Mr. Jameson leaned forward, his eyes locking with hers. "Esther, I know this is a lot to take in. But I also know that you have the strength, the intelligence, and the compassion to excel in this role. The decision is yours, but I have no doubt that you would make an extraordinary spokesperson for our city."

With those words, he placed the envelope on her desk and quietly took his leave, the door clicking shut behind him. Esther stared at the innocuous piece of paper, her heart pounding in her chest. She knew that the contents of that envelope held the power to change the course of her life, to set her on a path she had never dared to dream of.

And as she reached out with trembling fingers to grasp the envelope, Esther felt a surge of determination wash over her. Come what may, she would face this challenge with the same tenacity and grace that had brought her this far. For in this moment, she knew with unshakable certainty that her journey was only just beginning.

Get Esther: A Modern Tale of Love and Integrity now!

ABOUT THE AUTHOR

Award-winning author Kayla Lowe writes women's fiction that explores complex themes with sensitivity and depth. Kayla's books delve into the intricacies of relationships, self-discovery, and resilience. From cozy love stories interspersed with a bit of faith to heartwarming tales of friendship and suspenseful novels of empowerment and heartbreak, her books illustrate the struggles specific to women.

When she's not churning out her next novel, you can find her with her feet in the sand and a book in her hand or curled up on the couch with her dogs.

Visit her website at www.authorkaylalowe.com.

ALSO BY KAYLA LOWE

<u>Series</u>

<u>Charms of the Chaste Court</u>

A Courtship in Covent Garden

Whispers in Westminster

Romance in Regent's Park

Serenade on Strand Street

Treasure in Tower Bridge

<u>Sweet Honey by the Sea</u>

<u>The Beekeeper's Secret (Book 1)</u>

<u>A Royal Honeycomb (Book 2)</u>

<u>Bees in Blossom (Book 3)</u>

Honeyed Kisses (Book 4)

Blooming Forever (Book 5)

Strawberry Beach Series

Beachside Lessons (Book 1)

Beachside Lessons (Book 2)

Beachside Lessons (Book 3)

Panama City Beach Series

Sun-Kissed Secrets (Book 1)

Sun-Kissed Secrets (Book 2)

Sun-Kissed Secrets (Book 3)

The Tainted Love Saga

Of Love and Deception (Book 1)

Of Love and Family (Book 2)

Of Love and Violence (Book 3)

Of Love and Abuse(Book 4)

Of Love and Crime (Book 5)

Of Love and Addiction (Book 6)

Of Love and Redemption (Book 7)

<u>Standalones</u>

Maiden's Blush

<u>Poetry</u>

Phantom Poetry

Lost and Found